Magic Animal Friends

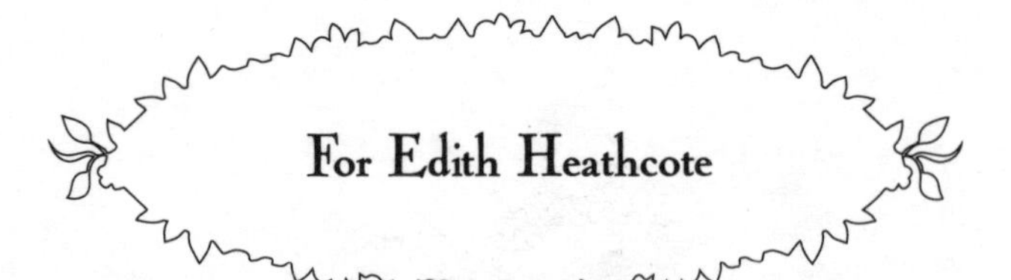

Special thanks to Conrad Mason

ORCHARD BOOKS

First published in Great Britain in 2017 by The Watts Publishing Group

1 3 5 7 9 10 8 6 4 2

A CIP catalogue record for this book is available from the British Library.

ISBN 978 1 40834 418 7

Printed in Great Britain

The paper and board used in this book are made from wood from responsible sources.

Orchard Books
An imprint of Hachette Children's Group
Part of The Watts Publishing Group Limited
Carmelite House, 50 Victoria Embankment, London EC4Y 0DZ

An Hachette UK Company
www.hachette.co.uk
www.hachettechildrens.co.uk

Sarah Scramblepaw's Big Step

Daisy Meadows

ORCHARD

Scramblepaws' Igloo

Grizelda's Lair

Littleleap Crossing Station

Fluffywhiskers Garden Station

Fluffywhiskers Garden

Fluffywhiskers Garden

Forest Halt Station

Forest Halt

Friendship Forest

Map of Magic Mountain
Littleleap Lodge
Orchard
Mines
Heppytail Cavern
The Friendship Express

Can you keep a secret? I thought you could!

Then I'll tell you about an enchanted wood.

It lies through the door in the old oak tree,

Let's go there now - just follow me!

We'll find adventure that never ends,

And meet the Magic Animal Friends!

Love,

Goldie the Cat

Contents

CHAPTER ONE

The Dancing Umbrella

"It's raining cats and dogs out there!" said Lily Hart, pulling on a pair of wellies by the back door of her kitchen. "We'd better help take the animals inside."

"Good idea," said Lily's best friend, Jess Forester. She picked up an umbrella with wide red and yellow stripes and together the girls hurried out into the downpour, sheltering under Jess's umbrella.

In the garden, the animals of Helping Paw Wildlife Hospital were huddled up inside their hutches. Lily's parents had set up the hospital, and she and Jess loved to help out whenever they could. Mr and Mrs Hart were already gathering up the bunnies, guinea pigs and hedgehogs to take indoors.

"Can you girls take the fox cubs in?" Mrs Hart called. "They're being a bit of a handful!"

She pointed to an open-air pen, where

some little fox cubs were wrestling and rolling on the muddy ground. They were soaked!

Jess unbolted the gate and Lily stepped into the pen. She bent down to scoop up a fox cub. But the little creature scurried away from her, waving his bushy tail.

"I think they're enjoying it!" said Jess,

laughing as another tiny fox cub squirmed out of her hands and jumped into a puddle with a splash.

Soon the girls had rounded up all the wriggling little foxes and carried them into the warm barn. As they went back outside again, a golden cat with green eyes that matched the wet grass ran towards them.

"Goldie!" said Lily and Jess at the same time.

Their special cat friend let out a soft purr in reply.

Jess gasped. "You know what this means," she said. "We're going to Friendship Forest!"

Lily's heart leapt with excitement. Friendship Forest was a magical place. The animals who lived there had tiny little cottages and could talk. And best of all, no one in the human world knew about Friendship Forest except Lily and Jess. Goldie the cat had taken them there for adventures many times before.

"I hope Grizelda isn't causing trouble again," said Lily, as they followed Goldie through the garden, hopping across

the stepping stones in the stream and into Brightley Meadow. Grizelda was an evil witch who kept trying to take over Friendship Forest and drive out the animals who lived there. But with Goldie's help, the girls had always managed to protect their animal friends.

"If she is, we'll stop her," said Jess. "And we'll be back in no time!"

The girls shared a smile. They both knew that time stood still while they were away in Friendship Forest.

Goldie stopped at a huge, dead old oak tree with bare branches. At once it burst

magically into life. Bright green leaves sprouted from its twigs. Its branches filled with shiny acorns. A little squirrel scurried up the trunk and disappeared through a hole, while a plump robin perched on the highest branch, puffing out his chest and singing sweetly. The Friendship Tree!

The girls knew just what to do next. They held hands and spoke the magic words carved into the tree trunk. "Friendship Forest!"

With a shimmer of sparkles, a tiny door formed in the trunk. The handle was shaped like a leaf, and when Jess turned it, the door creaked open. Golden light spilled from inside.

Lily propped her umbrella up against the trunk for safekeeping.

"Ready, Lily?" asked Jess.

"Ready, Jess!" said Lily.

Holding hands, the girls followed Goldie through the door. They felt a funny tingling as they shrank, just a little.

The golden light faded and they were

standing in a small, sunny clearing in the forest. A gentle breeze swayed the branches of the trees, and made the colourful flowers dance at their feet.

"I'm so pleased to see you two again," said a warm voice. Lily and Jess turned to see Goldie standing on her hind legs, a glittery scarf wrapped around her neck.

The girls smiled and gave Goldie a big hug.

"Is everything all right?" asked Jess, when they broke apart.

Goldie sighed. "I wish it was," she said. "Ranger Tuftybeard has seen Grizelda lurking about near Magic Mountain."

Magic Mountain was where all the magic of Friendship Forest was made. Grizelda wanted to stop the magic being made by stealing the special tools used to produce it. She had already tried three times, and the girls had stopped her.

"I have a nasty feeling she's up to no good again," said Goldie. "Will you help us?"

Lily and Jess looked at each other and nodded. "Of course we will!"

CHAPTER TWO

All Aboard!

Goldie led the girls straight to Forest Halt train station. The shiny red engine of the Friendship Express sat waiting on the rails, gently chugging away. Pretty pink wisps of candyfloss steam puffed out of its funnel.

"Howdy, partners!" called Ranger

Tuftybeard. The little white goat leaned out of the engine window, waving his hat. Lily was delighted to see the ranger. He knew Magic Mountain better than anyone, and was always helping the families who lived there.

"All aboard!" called Mr Whistlenose, the train driver. The little pug dog sat next to Ranger Tuftybeard, strapping on his goggles.

"I can't wait to ride through the forest again!" cheered Jess.

Goldie jumped into the carriage, and the girls followed, sitting next to Goldie in the puffy green and gold seats. The train whistle blew – TOOOOT! – and the Friendship Express huffed its way out of the station. "Next stop, Magic Mountain," called Ranger Tuftybeard. "Mighty fine to see you girls again!"

"Mighty fine to see you too!" Lily called back.

The girls settled back to watch the green trees of the forest whizzing by on either side. Candyfloss was streaming from the train funnel overhead. There was a gust of wind and a big puff of the candyfloss blew in through the window and into their faces.

They all giggled as they caught it and ate some. The girls loved the candyfloss steam!

"Let's save some for later," said Lily. Jess tore some pages from the sketchpad

she always kept in her pocket, and folded them up to make little parcels for the rest of the candyfloss. The girls tucked them into their pockets.

"Look!" called Goldie suddenly.

The girls peered up ahead, and spotted the beautiful green slopes and glittering snow cap of Magic Mountain rising high above the forest into the fluffy

white clouds. They felt a little thrill of excitement.

Soon the train was chugging steeply uphill.

Lily felt a tingling around her neck, and when she looked down she saw that she was wearing a pendant. It was the magical, petal-shaped crystal which Pippa Hoppytail, their rabbit friend, had given her. She held it up, so that it sparkled in the sunshine. "Look, Jess," she said. "You've got yours too!"

"So has Goldie," said Jess. "It must be the magic of the mountain!"

"Hang on to them, girls," said Goldie. "They might come in handy if we run into Grizelda." They knew Goldie was right. Lily's pendant could make things disappear, Jess's could transform things into different objects, and Goldie's could make things change colour.

"If we do see Grizelda, we could use them to disguise ourselves or to trick her," Lily said, tucking her pendant safely into her top.

They passed a rocky mine entrance where the Hoppytails lived, chugged past the pretty gardens which belonged to the Fluffywhiskers chipmunk family, and then up past the snowy rocks where the Littleleap goats were busy stirring crystals up to make a magical mixture.

The train slowed and Ranger Tuftybeard hopped off. He picked up a big bucket of sparkling magical mixture from the Littleleaps, then jumped back on to the train.

"So what happens at the top of the

mountain?" Lily asked. "We know the Hoppytails dig up the magic crystals from below the mountain."

"Yes, and the Fluffywhiskers family make them bigger by growing them in their garden." Jess added.

Goldie smiled. "That's right. When the Littleleaps dissolve the crystals to make the magical mixture, Ranger Tuftybeard takes it on up to the Scramblepaw family at the top of the mountain. They spread it all over Friendship Forest."

"How do the Scramblepaws do that?" asked Lily.

"You'll soon see," said Goldie, with a mysterious smile. Then her face fell. "As long as Grizelda and her troll servants haven't got there first."

The train kept going, higher and higher. Snow lay all around them on the rocks like icing on a birthday cake, dazzling white in the sunshine.

Then, the train whistle blew – *TOOOOT!* – and the engine came chugging to a stop. Ranger Tuftybeard leapt out and landed in the snow. "End of the line, girls," he called. "This is the very tip-top of Magic Mountain!"

Goldie and the girls waved goodbye to Mr Whistlenose the driver as they clambered off the train and followed Ranger Tuftybeard up the last steep slope, scrambling up to the peak of the mountain.

Even with snow all around, the air was magically warm. Soft little clouds bobbed all around them, but they could still see Friendship Forest far below, so small it looked like a patch of pretty green moss.

In front of them was a tiny igloo, made out of glittering ice. Next to it was a flat circle of rock, with a neat red X in the middle.

"That looks like a landing pad!" said Jess.

"The Scramblepaws have their own way of getting around," chuckled Goldie.

Then Lily caught sight of four little dots approaching through the sky. She peered closer, and saw four little white foxes. And each one was hanging on to a tiny umbrella!

"Here they are now!" cried Ranger Tuftybeard. "Look out, they're coming in to land!"

The first to arrive was Mr Scramblepaw, dangling from a purple umbrella. He floated down on to the red X and folded up his umbrella, whistling cheerfully. Next came Mrs Scramblepaw, drifting down on to the landing pad under a red umbrella with white spots. She landed next to Mr Scramblepaw.

Last of all came two fluffy little cubs, with the two tiniest yellow umbrellas that the girls had ever seen. As the littlest cub arrived, she took down her umbrella in mid-air, then did a nimble somersault and landed beside her parents with a small puff of snow.

The girls laughed and applauded, and the Scramblepaws all bowed together. The littlest cub scampered forward, waving her long bushy tail. "Hello there!" she squealed. "My name's Sarah, and this is my mum, my dad and my sister, Anna. We're the Scramblepaws! You must be Jess and Lily. It's lovely to meet you." She did a little back flip in excitement.

"It's lovely to meet you too," said Jess.

"You're a great acrobat, Sarah!"

Sarah beamed. "I love doing flips and

things. Especially when I've got my umbrella!"

"Your umbrellas are so pretty!" said Lily.

"They're very important too," said Mr Scramblepaw with a smile. "Without them, Friendship Forest wouldn't have any magic at all!"

"Why? What do you do with them?" asked Jess.

"We use them to fly up high above Friendship Forest," said Sarah. "Then we sprinkle the Littleleaps' magical mixture on to the clouds. After that we fly down

underneath the clouds and make it rain. The rain falls over all of Friendship Forest, and is soaked up by all the flowers and trees. That's what makes the forest magical."

Ranger Tuftybeard handed the bucket of magical mixture to Sarah. "Well, I'd best see how the other families are doing," he said, with a salute. Then he jumped back on the train. Lily and Jess waved goodbye, as the engine began to chug its way back down the mountain.

"More magical mixture!" squeaked Sarah, hugging the bucket tight. "Would you like to see how we turn it into magical rain?"

"Yes please!" said Lily and Jess together.

Then Jess gasped and pointed into the sky. A sickly yellow-green orb of light was floating towards them. Then it exploded in a sudden shower of smelly green sparks. *BANG!*

Where the light had been stood a lanky figure, dressed in a shiny purple tunic and a black cloak, with long green hair flying out in the breeze.

"Oh no," cried Sarah. "It's Grizelda!"

CHAPTER THREE

Troll Trouble

"Well, look who's here!" sneered Grizelda. "It's the pesky girls and the silly cat. You'd better stay out of my way – and you too, foxes! Friendship Forest will soon be mine!"

"The forest will never be yours," said Lily sternly. "It belongs to the animals."

Grizelda threw back her head and cackled. "That's what you think! But once I've stopped those silly animals from making their magic, they'll have to leave the forest. Without magic there'll be no more magical food! No more magical flowers! No more nasty, horrible, rotten fun!"

"Oh dear," whispered Sarah, clinging on to Jess's leg. "She doesn't like anything nice, does she?"

"Don't worry," Jess told the little fox cub. "Whatever she's planning, she won't get away with it."

"Oh, won't I?" snarled Grizelda. She raised her hand, and four green bolts of magic shot from her fingertips. They sizzled into the snow and sent up four puffs of green smoke.

When the smoke cleared, her four troll servants were standing there, dusting themselves off. They looked like little piles of

boulders, with tough grey skin.

"Me hungry troll," grumbled Rocky, rubbing his belly.

"Me more hungry!" said Flinty. He held up a crumbly grey biscuit and looked at it sadly. "Rock cakes not yum yum."

"Grizelda give us tasty nosh?" asked Craggy, a troll with spiky white hair.

"Yes yes!" added Pebble.

"Silence, the lot of you!" Grizelda snapped at the trolls. "You'll get nothing till you've stolen those flying umbrellas!"

Lily and Jess looked at each other in shock. But before they could do anything, the trolls had bounded across the snow. They shoved the girls and Goldie out of the way and snatched all four umbrellas from the Scramblepaws.

Grizelda cackled in triumph as her servants raced off through the snow. "You can't make magic now, can you?" she taunted. "So long, pests!" Then she disappeared in a shower of green sparks.

"Quick! We can't let them get away!" Jess cried.

Lily, Jess and Goldie ran off through the snow, following the big clumsy footprints

left behind by the trolls. They hadn't got far when a voice called out to them.

"Wait for me!"

They glanced back and saw that little Sarah Scramblepaw was chasing after them, her pointy white ears pricked up with excitement. "I'm not scared of those smelly old trolls," said Sarah breathlessly.

"I'm going to help you save Friendship Forest. Mum and Dad said I could."

Lily grinned. "What a brave little cub!"

The four of them ran on together, and soon the trolls came back into sight, lumbering through the snow just ahead. "Stop right there!" Jess shouted to them.

Craggy yelped and sped up. "Quick!" he cried. "Trolls go to Grizelda's secret lair, like she said!" He opened Mr Scramblepaw's purple umbrella, and immediately floated up off the snow. The other trolls opened their umbrellas too, and soon all four of them were drifting through the sky. Pebble blew a raspberry back at Goldie, and the next moment they had all disappeared behind a cloud.

Sarah tried to jump up and catch hold of them, but she missed and landed with a graceful roll.

"What now?" said Jess, as they came panting to a halt. "We can't fly without the umbrellas."

"Or maybe we can," said Lily thoughtfully. She put her hands together and opened and closed them like wings.

"Oh yes!" said Jess. "We can call the butterflies to help us." She joined in

flapping her hands. "But then what?"

Lily smiled as, almost at once, a delicate little blue butterfly came fluttering to land on her fingertips. "Hello there," said the butterfly. "I'm Barnaby. Can I help?"

"Yes please, Barnaby," said Lily. "Can you write out a message, Jess? It's for Mr Cleverfeather. He's such a brilliant

inventor – if anyone can find a way for us to fly, it's him."

"Good idea," said Goldie, as Jess pulled her sketchpad from her pocket.

She scribbled away with a pencil, then tore the page out, rolled it up and offered it to the butterfly. "Can you give this to our owl friend Mr Cleverfeather? It's very urgent," she said.

"Don't worry," said Barnaby. "I'm the fastest butterfly on the mountain! I'll find him in no time."

"I hope he's right," said Lily, as the little creature carried Jess's message off into the air. "If we don't get after those trolls soon, we'll never catch them!"

"Then Friendship Forest will run out of magic for ever!" exclaimed Goldie.

CHAPTER FOUR

Whizzy Wings

Luckily, they didn't have to wait long.

"Is that him?" cried Sarah, a few minutes later.

Mr Cleverfeather the owl came hovering down from the sky in his Helicopter Harness, his monocle glinting in the sunshine. He dropped a big brown

bag on to the snow – FLUMPF! – then landed beside it, adjusting his little waistcoat with his wings. "Goodness me, what a delight. Less and Jilly! Er, I mean, Jess and Lily! How are you?"

Lily couldn't hold in a giggle. Mr Cleverfeather was always muddling up his words.

"We need your help, Mr Cleverfeather. Grizelda's trolls have flown off with the

Scramblepaw family's magic umbrellas!"

"We stust mop her!" said Mr Cleverfeather. "I mean, must stop her." He opened his bag and drew out four sets of glittery wings with straps. Mr Cleverfeather handed one to each of the girls, one to Sarah and one to Goldie. "There you are," he said. "They're my latest invention. I call them Whizzy Wings."

Jess, Lily, Goldie and Sarah all pulled the wings on.

"They're beautiful," said Jess. "But how do they work?"

"Easy!" said the inventor owl. "To take off you simply tell them, 'Whizzy Wings, do your thing', and prey hesto! I mean, hey presto!"

"Whizzy Wings, do your thing," Lily told her wings. To her amazement, the Whizzy Wings began to flutter with a humming sound, and her feet left the snow as she floated upwards.

The others copied her, and soon all four of them were hovering in the air.

"Thank you so much, Mr Cleverfeather!" said Lily.

"Helighted to delp!" said Mr Cleverfeather. "I mean ... oh, never mind. Good luck!"

Jess, Lily, Goldie and Sarah waved and flew off, their Whizzy Wings buzzing. Sarah twirled in the air and did a somersault. The girls darted in and out of the clouds, their hair flying back in the breeze. It was so much fun, but they knew they had to concentrate. They had to find Grizelda's trolls before it was too late.

As they burst through a big cloud, Goldie let out a gasp. "Oh, no ... The Friendship Tree!"

Lily's heart sank when she looked down and saw the big green forest below. Right in the middle, the Friendship Tree looked strange and see-through. The leaves at the ends of the branches had almost

completely faded away.

"What's happening?" asked Jess.

"The magic of Friendship Forest is running out," said Sarah. Her whiskers drooped. "And that's what gives the Friendship Tree life. If we don't get those umbrellas back soon, the Friendship Tree will disappear entirely."

"And if there's no Friendship Tree, we won't be able to get home," said Jess.

"That's right," said Goldie sadly. "Friendship Forest will be cut off from your world for ever!"

"Then we must find those trolls," said Lily, with determination. "And we'd better be quick, before the magic of the Whizzy Wings runs out too."

They looked all around, but it was hard to see past the fluffy clouds scudding through the sky.

"Lily, your pendant!" said Jess suddenly.

"Of course!" Lily reached up to the

crystal hanging round her neck. "We can use its magic to make the clouds invisible. Then we can see through them and find the trolls!" She closed her hand over the pendant and spoke the magic words. "Crystal flower, show your power!"

The pendant sparkled with magic, and at once the clouds became see-through. All except one.

"That's strange," said Goldie, peering at the only cloud left in the sky. It was big, dark and gloomy, quite different from the rest of the clouds, which were soft, white and puffy.

They flew closer, their Whizzy Wings buzzing.

"Is that a door?" said Jess, pointing.

Lily gasped. Sure enough, right in the middle of the cloud there was a little wooden door, painted entirely black. "Do you remember what those trolls said when they flew off?" she murmured.

"They said they were going to Grizelda's secret lair," said Jess. "And I think we've found it!"

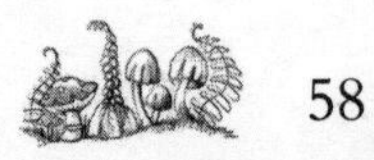

CHAPTER FIVE

The Candyfloss Caper

Poor little Sarah was trembling, and her big eyes were open wide. "Do you think that mean old witch will be in there?" she said.

"She might be," said Lily gently, stroking her. "But we promise to look after you, whatever happens."

Sarah snuggled in close to Lily's side. "Oh, thank you! I won't be so scared if I'm with you."

Lily and Jess looked at each other. They knew they needed to be brave to save their friends.

Goldie turned the handle, and the black door creaked open. Then the four of them flew inside and landed on a floor that felt soft and squishy, like a marshmallow. Looking around, they found that they were in a dark, dank hallway.

Sarah jumped up and down on the bouncy floor. "It's all made out of some

kind of
magical
storm cloud!"

"A storm cloud sounds like Grizelda's magic, all right," said Lily.

"We'd better take our Whizzy Wings off," Jess said. "We don't want the trolls to hear us." They each shrugged off their wings, which stopped buzzing at once, and tucked them under the doormat.

"Wait – do you hear something?" Jess

whispered to her friends.

They all stayed very quiet, and after a moment they heard voices coming from somewhere inside the cloud.

"I think it's the trolls," said Goldie. "We'd better investigate."

Lily and Jess led the way, creeping along the dark corridor. It twisted and turned, taking them deeper into Grizelda's lair.

As they rounded a bend, Jess jumped in shock, then held the others back.

Cautiously, Lily peered round the corner. She saw a big room with wooden

furniture, all painted black. Sitting in a black rocking chair was Grizelda. Her four trolls stood in front of her, each holding an umbrella.

"It's them! It's the trolls!" said Sarah excitedly.

"Shh!" whispered Jess.

Sarah clapped her little white paws over

her muzzle, looking terrified again.

"Tummy growly," moaned Flinty.

"Rock cakes gone," groaned Rocky.

"We go forest, find food?" asked Pebble.

"Animals got fruit tarts," added Craggy. "Jelly and cakes! Om-nom-nom!"

"Enough!" growled Grizelda. "You're giving me a headache! You'll get something to eat when I've taken over the forest, and not before! Now, lock those umbrellas up, so those meddling girls and animals will never find them."

The witch rose and tossed the trolls a large metal key. Then, with a swish of

her cape, she swept out of the room. Still grumbling about food, the trolls went to a large black cupboard, opened it and put the umbrellas inside.

"What shall we do?" whispered Goldie.

"I've got it!" said Jess. "Those trolls want some tasty food, don't they? Well, we've got some in our pockets."

"Candyfloss!" said Lily. "Of course!"

Lily and Jess reached into their pockets and drew out the paper parcels of candyfloss they had taken from the train.

"We'll distract the trolls," said Jess. "Goldie can keep a lookout, and Sarah, you grab the umbrellas."

"You can count on me!" said Sarah, puffing out her chest.

Lily and Jess tiptoed up behind the trolls, as quietly as they could. Then they tore the candyfloss into pieces and laid a little trail leading across the floor, away from the cupboard. Finally they hid behind

Grizelda's rocking chair, where the trolls couldn't see them.

"Mmm, candyfloss!" Lily said loudly, in her best troll voice.

Jess had to clamp her mouth shut to stop herself from giggling.

Pebble turned to look. "Who say that?" he growled. Then he saw the candyfloss, and his eyes opened wide. "Om-nom-nom!" The other trolls turned too, and with whoops of excitement they fell on the trail of pink candy, gobbling it up piece by piece.

Jess waved a hand, and Sarah leapt into

action. She did a nimble somersault across the floor. Then she curled her tail around all four umbrellas, which were sitting inside the open cupboard. She kept the

umbrellas held tightly in her tail as she ran back to the others.

"Well done, Sarah!" whispered Lily.

"Let's get out of here!" added Jess.

The girls and Sarah raced across the floor towards Goldie. But Goldie let out a sudden gasp of shock and pointed behind them. The girls stopped in their tracks and spun round.

Grizelda had returned. Her green hair was waving like a nest of snakes, and she was scowling furiously. "Trying to spoil my plans again, are we?" she roared. "Well, since you girls like candyfloss so much, you'd better prepare for a sticky end!" She raised her fingers, and began to chant. "*Grumble, rumble, crack and crumble, make these fools from my lair tumble* ..."

"Uh-oh," said Jess. "She's casting a spell."

The girls hugged Goldie and Sarah tightly, as the witch flung out her hands …

CHAPTER SIX

Troll Pancakes

Ffffzzzzzzzzzzzap!

A little shower of green sparks spilled from Grizelda's fingertips and fell harmlessly on to the floor. The witch scowled and jabbed her hands again. This time there wasn't so much as a fizzle.

"Bristling broomsticks!" screeched

Grizelda. "It's not working!" She stamped her foot, but still nothing happened.

"Of course," whispered Lily. "The magic is running out all over Friendship Forest – even Grizelda's! She can't cast her wicked spells any more."

"That does it," snapped the witch. "Flinty! Rocky! Craggy! Pebble! After them!"

The girls dashed out of the room, with Goldie and Sarah running beside them. Behind, they could hear the clumping footsteps of the trolls.

"Run!" panted Jess.

But the dark corridor had begun to shimmer all around them. Then sunshine burst through as the walls and floor started to fade away.

"Oh dear," said Goldie. "Grizelda's lair is made of magic too."

"It's disappearing!" gasped Lily.

"Quick, take these!" said Sarah. She handed an umbrella to Goldie, then one to each of the girls.

"But won't they have lost their magic too?" Jess asked.

Sarah shook her head. "My mum and dad say they're the only things in the

forest that don't need the magical rain. They're always magical!"

The next moment there was nothing left of the floor, and they all tumbled downwards. Lily heard an angry screech above, and she spotted a ball of yellow-green light streaking away through the sky. Even Grizelda's magical orb was much dimmer than usual.

"Open your umbrellas, girls!" called Goldie.

Lily and Jess opened them. *WHUMPH!* The magical umbrellas caught the wind at once. Lily felt herself slowing, then

gently rising upwards. She looked down and saw the tops of the trees not far below her feet. "Phew!" she gasped, as she saw Jess, Goldie and Sarah floating upwards under their own umbrellas.

"What about the trolls?" cried Sarah suddenly.

The trolls were still falling towards the forest, waving their arms and legs wildly.

"We've got to rescue them!" said Lily. "Come on, umbrella, let's go!"

Lily's umbrella swooped through the air. Hanging on with one hand, she reached out with the other and caught Pebble's wrist. The umbrella swayed with the extra weight. Then it drifted slowly down in between the trees.

Lily and Pebble landed gently in a clearing, on the soft green grass of the forest floor. Lily closed up her umbrella as her friends arrived too, each with a troll dangling below.

"That was close," said Jess when they

had all landed safely.

"We almost troll pancakes!" said Pebble.

"No talk pancakes," said Flinty, rubbing his belly. "Me still hungry!"

"You help us," said Rocky to the girls.

"We help you now," said Craggy. "What we do?"

"Well, you could stop doing everything Grizelda says," said Lily. "She isn't being very kind to the animals of Friendship Forest. And I don't think she's being very kind to you either."

"You right," said Pebble. "She not give us tasty yums."

"She call us mean names," added Rocky.

"We no help her again!" said Craggy.

"It's agreed, then!" said Jess, with a smile. "Now, you should go to the Toadstool Café. There's lots of lovely food there. We'll come and join you, but first we've got to get these umbrellas back to the Scramblepaws."

"Hooray!" said Sarah, bouncing up and down, her bushy white tail waving happily. "Mum and Dad will be so pleased!"

Holding the umbrellas high, they took

off again and floated above the forest. Lily spotted the Friendship Tree. Even more of the leaves had faded away. It looked more like a shadow than a tree. "The magic has almost gone!" she cried.

"Let's just hope we aren't too late to help," said Goldie.

Soon afterwards, Sarah, Goldie and the girls came drifting down on to the neat red X at the summit of Magic Mountain.

They were just closing their umbrellas when Mr Scramblepaw poked his head out of the little igloo. "Hooray!" he cried.

"I knew you'd get them back!"

He came rushing out with Mrs Scramblepaw and Sarah's sister, and all three of them pulled Sarah, Goldie and the girls into a big hug.

"We're so proud of you!" cooed Mrs Scramblepaw, stroking her daughter's head.

Sarah smiled shyly. "It wasn't just me.

We did it together!"

"Thank you so much, girls and Goldie," said Mr Scramblepaw. "You've saved Friendship Forest."

"You're welcome," said Jess. "But the forest still needs its magic, and quickly!"

"Quite right," said Mrs Scramblepaw. "Now we've got our umbrellas back, we can fly up to where we sprinkle the magical mixture over the clouds. Perhaps you girls would like to do it this time?"

Lily and Jess grinned. "Yes, please!"

"Come on," said Sarah. "I'll show you!"

CHAPTER SEVEN

Magical Rain

Sarah darted into the igloo and came out a moment later with two silver watering cans. She gave one to Lily and one to Jess. Lily peered inside and saw a shimmering, rainbow-coloured liquid. Bubbles danced across the surface, bursting with sprays of brilliant colour.

"That's the magical mixture," said Sarah. She opened up her umbrella and floated off the snow. "Now follow me!"

The girls flew after the little fox cub, with Goldie at their side. Sarah led them up above the clouds. Lily and Jess took turns sprinkling a little mixture on to each one, until every cloud was sparkling with magic.

"Perfect!" said Sarah. "Now all we

need to do is fly underneath and make it rain." She swooped down beneath the clouds. Goldie and the girls followed, swishing through the air.

At once, shimmering raindrops began to fall, pattering gently on their umbrellas. Lily held out her hand and felt the cool splash of the rain. Every droplet glittered with a thousand colours, just like the magical crystals they had seen further down the mountain.

"Come on!" called Goldie, as she and Sarah flew down the mountainside. Lily and Jess followed, soaring above

Friendship Forest and skimming the treetops. The trees seemed to be standing taller and greener, sparkling in the magical rain. Jess pointed at the Friendship Tree, and Lily's heart leapt as she saw that it was as solid and leafy as ever.

"We did it," murmured Jess.

"Nothing can stop us coming back to Friendship Forest now!" said Lily.

"Well done, girls," said Goldie, smiling. "You've saved the magic of the forest for all of us." She flew closer with her umbrella and swept the girls into a tight hug in midair.

"And now," said Goldie, when they broke apart, "I think it's high time for a celebration!"

Soon afterwards, beneath the sparkling rain, Toadstool Glade buzzed with cheerful voices, music and laughter. Delicious treats were laid out inside the Toadstool Café – a gigantic lavender cream cake, gooey rainbow cookies and, of course, candyfloss from the Friendship Express.

The animals were having a wonderful time eating and drinking, splashing in the puddles and sticking their tongues out to catch raindrops. Ranger Tuftybeard had come with all four of the families from Magic Mountain. Even the four trolls were there. They were playing hide and seek with the youngest animals, pretending to be rocks, then whooping with excitement and running away when they were found.

Lily and Jess couldn't help grinning at the sight of their animal friends having so much fun.

Sarah did a somersault and landed with her mouth wide open, catching the

TOADSTOOL
CAFE

raindrops on her little pink tongue. The girls clapped and Sarah said "Try the rain! It's delicious!"

Jess stuck her tongue out and caught a raindrop. "It tastes like mango sorbet!" she gasped.

Lily put out her tongue too. "This drop is vanilla milkshake!" she said.

"That's because the rain is magical," said Goldie. "Every drop has a different taste!"

"This is such a lovely party," said Jess, grinning. "And for once there's no Grizelda to ruin things."

Just then, a bright yellow-green orb appeared through the trees. The animals froze, trembling and looking up at it nervously. Some of them scurried over to hide behind Lily and Jess.

"I think we spoke too soon," said Lily,

her heart sinking.

With a loud CRACK, Grizelda appeared in a shower of smelly sparks.

CHAPTER EIGHT

A Nice Hew Nome

The animals cowered in fright as Grizelda stamped her foot and scowled at the girls. "You think you're so clever, don't you? Well, this isn't over! My trolls will snatch all the magical umbrellas back, and then Friendship Forest will be mine at last!"

The Scramblepaw family huddled

behind Lily and Jess. "I'm scared!" murmured Sarah.

"Don't worry," said Lily. "I have a feeling Grizelda's plan isn't going to work."

"What are you waiting for?" Grizelda snapped at the trolls. "Go on! Steal their umbrellas!"

The trolls all hung their heads, trying

not to look at the witch.

"Animals give candyfloss," said Pebble.

"Cookies too!" added Flinty.

"No yucky rock cakes," said Craggy.

"We like animals," said Rocky. "They friendly. We no take their magic away."

"You know, the magic helps everyone, Grizelda," said Jess.

"That's not the point!" screeched the witch.

"It even helps you," said

Lily. "You couldn't do any spells without magic, could you?"

"I ... er ... well ..." The witch's face went deep red. "Fine! Those pests can keep their stinky magic. But I'm still going to take over the forest. Just you wait ..." Then, with another shower of green sparks, she disappeared.

"Good riddance," said Jess.

"Hooray!" chanted the animals. "Lily and Jess saved us again!"

"Well done, girls," said Goldie. "Now, let's enjoy the party!"

The girls danced in the rain with their

animal friends, then ate their fill of cake and cookies. Before they knew it, dusk was falling.

"Where we go now?" said a sad little voice. Lily turned and saw the four trolls kicking their heels gloomily in the corner of the garden. "No Grizelda, no home," said Pebble.

"Perhaps I can help," said Mr Cleverfeather the owl. He shuffled forward, carrying a pile of his inventions.

"Our Whizzy Wings!" said Jess.

"Yes indeed," said Mr Cleverfeather. "They fell right on top of my treehouse, you know!" He handed the wings to the trolls. "There – now you can fly up into the mountains where there are lots of caves, and find yourselves a nice hew nome!"

"What is nome?" said Flinty suspiciously.

"Mr Cleverfeather means a nice new

home," Lily explained.

"Goody!" said Craggy.

"Here, have some cake for the journey," said Goldie. She wrapped up some slices of lavender cream cake in napkins and passed them round.

The trolls bounced up and down with excitement. "Thank girls! Thank cat!" they cried together. They pulled on their wings, and soon they were whizzing off into the distance.

"I think it's time we were going too," said Lily.

"Goodbye!" called Sarah. "I won't

forget you, Jess and Lily!"

"We won't forget you, either," Jess promised. "I'm sure we'll see you again."

Goldie walked with them to the Friendship Tree and hugged them both. "Thank you both so much for your help," she said. "You have saved Friendship Forest once again."

The girls waved goodbye to their friendand stepped through the little door into the golden light.

It was still raining when Lily and Jess stepped out of the little door in the oak tree, back into Brightley Meadow. Jess's stripy umbrella leant against the trunk, just where she had left it, and the girls sheltered underneath it as they hopped over the stepping stones back into the garden.

Jess jumped into a puddle with a big splash, then held out her tongue to catch a raindrop. "It isn't quite as yummy as the Friendship Forest rain," she said, with a laugh.

They hurried back to check on the animals in the barn. The little fox cubs had finally settled down, except for the smallest, who was still tumbling and rolling around the hutch!

"He's quite an acrobat." said Lily.

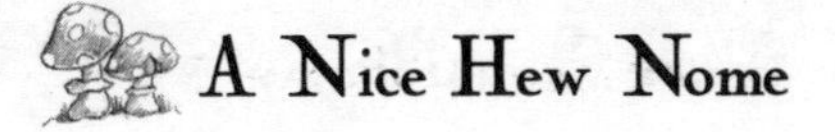

"Just like Sarah Scramblepaw!" replied Jess, with a smile.

The girls left the barn and slipped into Lily's kitchen through the back door. Lily's mum was holding two steaming mugs of hot chocolate.

"Yum! Thanks, Mrs Hart," said Jess, taking the mugs.

"You're welcome," said Mrs Hart. "I bet you girls are glad to be out of that rain."

Lily and Jess looked at each

 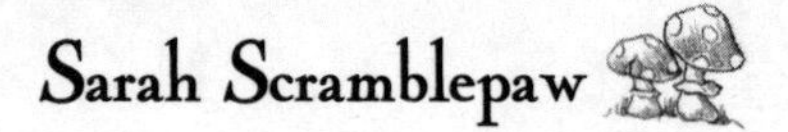

other and smiled.

"Actually, Mum," said Lily, "we think the rain is totally magical!"

The End

The animals of Friendship Forest are getting ready for a sports day! But wicked Grizelda wants to spoil the fun. Can Lily and Jess help super-cute kitten Anna Fluffyfoot stop the witch's horrible plans?

Find out in the next Magic Animal Friends Special,

Anna Fluffyfoot Goes for Gold

Turn over for a sneak peek ...

"The stable looks fantastic!" Lily Hart said to her best friend, Jess Forester.

Lily's parents ran the Helping Paw Wildlife Hospital in a barn in their garden, and the girls adored working with the poorly animals. Today they were helping Mr and Mrs Hart in a field behind the garden where there was a paddock with a stable. They'd just finished putting down a bed of wood shavings.

"It's great!" said Jess. "Starshine Sparkle's going to love it!"

Starshine Sparkle was a retired racehorse who belonged to a man in the local village. Now she wasn't racing any more, the stable would be her new home.

Mrs Hart smiled and pointed to the garden over the fence. "We've got an audience!"

The animals in the hospital's outdoor pens were watching curiously. Three baby rabbits peeped out from their hutch. In the next pen, a tiny squirrel sat in her feed bowl to watch. A white goat kid and a caramel-coloured calf stood beneath a shady tree, keeping an eye on the activity.

Lily laughed. "Starshine Sparkle will have lots of company here!"

Mr Hart brought over a water bucket. "Starshine Sparkle's owner, Tom, says he'll visit her whenever he can," he said. "She's got a lovely paddock to gallop around, so she'll be perfectly happy."

Mrs Hart closed the stable door. "We'll sweep up," she said, looking at the hay wisps blowing about. "You girls have worked so hard. Off you go – enjoy this lovely summer day!"

"Thanks, Mum!" said Lily.

"See you!" said Jess.

"Racehorses must have exciting lives," said Lily, as they walked across the garden towards the house. "If only Starshine Sparkle could talk, like the animals in Friendship Forest!"

Read

Anna Fluffyfoot Goes for Gold

to find out what happens next!

Can Jess and Lily save the magic of
Friendship Forest from Grizelda?
Read all of series six to find out!

COMING SOON!
Look out for
Jess and Lily's
next adventure:
Anna Fluffyfoot Goes for Gold!

www.magicanimalfriends.com

Jess and Lily's Animal Facts

Lily and Jess love lots of different animals – both in Friendship Forest and in the real world.

Here are their top facts about

ARCTIC FOXES

like Sarah Scramblepaw:

- Arctic foxes have incredibly thick fur all over their body, even on the base of their paws! This allows them to walk on both snow and ice.

- Their bushy tails help to keep them warm in extremely low temperatures – sometimes as low as minus 58 degrees!

- The fur of an Arctic fox changes with the seasons. During the winter it is white so they can be camouflaged in the snow, but in the summer it changes to brown.

- The Arctic fox is the only native land mammal in Iceland. Other animals have either made their own way to Iceland over time or have been introduced by humans.